Chasing Sunsets

written by
KENDRA ANDRUS

illustrated by
SORINEL CÂRSTIUC

Can you spot a turtle in every picture?

For my 6 Muses

Willow, Wilder, Chapel, Aria, Arow, and *EdenPearl*

*You all light up my world and bring
much adventure and awe!*

Never stop chasing sunsets — and finding God.

I love you too much.

Sometimes my mommy
gets a twinkle in her eye
and she jumps up and sings:

"We need to imagine,
dance, and fly!"

It's usually because we are
grouchy,
restless,
or worn out

It's usually because we need
adventure,
and a happy reason
to shout.

So she hurries us all to put our shoes on and then

We climb into the car, without knowing
where, what, or when

She turns the key and away we go
　　Down the street with a laugh and a to and a fro
It just so happens that the sky is beginning
　　To turn colors and highlight the clouds that are spinning

"We are racing!" she cries,
    as the lights are all shining

"To catch the sunset!"
    as it paints the horizon

All through the neighborhood
we dash and we cruise

As we chase the sunset
with its colorful hues

The best place to witness
the incredible sight

Is on top of a hill,
nothing blocking the light

We drive and we turn
on every road we believe

Will take us to the
perfect spot
that we won't
want to leave

We try to avoid tall trees
and houses and valleys

As we play pick-a-road,
pick-a-street, pick-an-alley

"The sky, she's a-changing,"
  Mom yells out with full heart

"We'd better be quick
  or we'll miss the best part!"

My mommy she cries:
"Look at that beautiful sky!"

While we wiggle and wind
through the streets low and high

We point in the same direction and all of us shout
"Go *that* way! We feel it!" And she turns without a doubt

The sunset will last just
a short time and, too,

The look of it will change
every second or few

So our eyes are all open
not once will we blink

For fear of missing a moment
of the explosion of ink!

There is beauty
and mystery
and artistic design

In the colors
that line up
and stain the skyline

And there we settle
as we all hold our breath

We've done it! We've done it!
We've caught the sunset!

She rolls down the windows
and turns off the van

Then we all pop our heads out,
proud we did it again

Our big brother, he makes the first move like a goof

And the next thing my mom knows,
We're all up on the roof!

We sit and look up
as we stare high above...

...and we imagine we're swimming
in the colors of love

Pinks and purples and oranges,
yellows and grays

With the fluff
of the clouds

and the blue
that
still
stays

Our mission is accomplished
and we all are in awe

Of the fun of the chase
and the God who can draw

Perfect pictures just for us
to know God's never done

Giving us pleasure and joy,
adventure and fun

Our big sister, she sighs
with a gleam in her eye

As she says, "Thank you God
for Your awesome art in the sky!"

the

end

About the Author

Kendra Andrus is a homeschooling mother who finds endless inspiration for children's books in her everyday life with her own six children. She writes to solve their problems, answer their questions, and tell the stories of their adventures together. She loves Jesus, teaching, cooking, reading, art, poetry, dancing, and singing. Together, she and her husband manage the loud and feisty-fun chaos that is their daily life in Nashville, Tennessee.

About the Illustrator

Sorinel Cârstiuc graduated from the University of Fine Arts in Iasi, Romania. He is currently a professor at the Art High School "Hadirclea Darclee" in Braila, Romania. He founded the "Bellart Atelier Creativ," a workshop for children and teens. He has participated in many art projects and exhibitions.

Acknowledgements

Thank you to the two best word-crafters in the world: my parents (and editors), Mark and Susan Davis. I love the magic of language and have learned to use it well because of you.

Thank you to my husband Matthew, who endures a home overflowing with books and who supported our investment in my own pursuit of authoring them. Thank you for believing in them and in me.

Enormous appreciation goes to my talented sister Heather for her design and formatting efforts — she used love and skill to create a beautiful finished product.

And cheers to Brenda Carroll: every author needs someone to push her beyond what she thought herself capable of. Thank you for showing me the way.

Much thanks to the following friends and family who also believed in me and in this venture, and who gave generously to make it happen:
Jayce and Nicole Nichols, Paul and Terra Davis, Harper and Haven Davis, Evan Stern, Ashley Atkins, Tommy Britt, and Meredith and Chalmer Harper.

And to all the children who will hold and explore and interact with this book: may you forever enjoy the life inside of books and may your lives be different and better for spending time in them. You are loved.

CPSIA information can be obtained at www.ICGtesting.com
Printed in the USA
LVIW01n0609211217
560428LV00007B/60